DATE DUE			

E
HOW

Howe, James.

The day the teacher
went bananas.

Resource Center
Everett Dirksen School
116 W. Beech Drive
Schaumburo IL 60193

SCHAUMBURG SCHOOL DISTRICT #54

The Day
the Teacher Went
Bananas

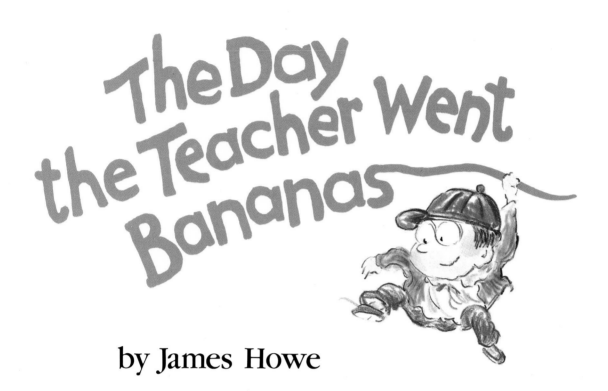

The Day the Teacher Went Bananas

by James Howe

illustrated by Lillian Hoban

E. P. DUTTON • NEW YORK

Published in the United States by E. P. Dutton,
2 Park Avenue, New York, N.Y. 10016,
a division of NAL Penguin Inc.

Published simultaneously in Canada by
Fitzhenry & Whiteside Limited, Toronto

Editor: Ann Durell Designer: Isabel Warren-Lynch

Printed in Hong Kong by South China Printing Co.
10 9 8 7 6 5 4   COBE

Library of Congress Cataloging in Publication Data

Howe, James.
     The day the teacher went bananas.

     Summary: A class's new teacher, who leads the
children in a number of very popular activities,
turns out to be a gorilla.
     [I. Teachers—Fiction.   2. Schools—Fiction.
3. Gorillas—Fiction]   I. Hoban, Lillian, ill.   II. Title.
PZ7.H83727Day   1984   [E]   84-1536
ISBN 0-525-44107-7

for my mother

One day a new teacher arrived
at our school.

We didn't know what to call him,
because he wouldn't tell us his
name. He just grunted a lot.

When it was time for arithmetic, he
showed us how to count on our toes.

And we learned a new way to write.

We went outside for science class.

Then we went back inside for lunch.
The teacher ate sixteen bananas.

"Tomorrow, let's bring bananas for
lunch," we all said, wanting to be
just like our new teacher.

Then we had art class. Our teacher
taught us how to work with clay.

And paper.

And paint.

Then we studied music.

Suddenly, Mr. Hornsby, the school
principal, came into the room with
another man.

"There has been a terrible mix-up,"
Mr. Hornsby said. "This isn't
your new teacher. This is
a gorilla."

The man with Mr. Hornsby said, "I am your new teacher. My name is Mr. Quackerbottom. I was sent to the zoo by mistake."

Sadly, we all waved good-bye
to the gorilla.

"Now," Mr. Quackerbottom said, "what have you learned today?"

We showed him.

"Why, this is awful!" Mr. Quackerbottom
cried. "You all belong in the zoo!"

And the next day, that's exactly where we went...

... to have lunch with our
favorite teacher.